Winnie the Pooh
and the Honey Tree

Adapted by **Mary Packard**
Illustrated by **Russell Hicks**

A GOLDEN BOOK • NEW YORK
Golden Books Publishing Company, Inc., New York, New York 10106

Winnie the Pooh was sitting by the stove in his best armchair when his Pooh Coo clock began to chime.

"*Pooh Coo, Pooh Coo,*" it said.

As soon as he heard it, Pooh knew it was time for something. And when his tummy began to growl, the little bear knew exactly what it was.

"It's time for something sweet," said Pooh. So off he went to the cupboard where he kept his honey jar.

"Oh, bother," said Pooh as he lifted the jar from the shelf. "Empty again! Only the sticky part's left."

Just then a bee flew in through the window and landed on Pooh's ear. Pooh listened thoughtfully to the buzzing little bee.

"The only reason for making a buzzing noise that I know of is because you're a . . . a bee," said Pooh. "And the only reason for being a bee . . . is to make honey. And the only reason for making honey is so I can eat it!" he concluded with a chuckle.

Pooh followed the bee out the door of his home and through the Hundred-Acre Wood. And when he came to a honey tree, he began to climb it.

As Pooh climbed the tree, he sang a little song to himself. It went something like this:

"When I'm rumbly in my tummy,
It's time to get some honey.
But I wouldn't climb a tree
If I could fly just like a bee!"

Pooh climbed a little higher . . . and then higher still.

He was just about to reach for the honey when the branch he was sitting on went CRACK!

"Oh, help!" cried Pooh as he began to fall. "If only I hadn't . . .You see, what I meant to do . . ."

But by this time Pooh had already hit the ground with a *thump*! As Pooh brushed the prickles from his nose, he decided that he needed help in getting the honey. And his good friend Christopher Robin would be just the person to help him.

So Winnie the Pooh went to look for his friend. He
found him outside his house in another part of the Wood.
"Good morning, Christopher Robin," he said. Then
he noticed a balloon tied to Christopher Robin's tricycle.
It gave Pooh a wonderful idea.
"I wonder if you've got such a thing as a balloon about
you?" hinted the bear.
"What for?" asked Christopher Robin.

Pooh looked this way and that. When he was sure
that nobody was listening, he whispered, "Honey!"
    "How do you get honey with a balloon?" asked the boy.
    "I shall fly like a bee," replied Pooh. "Up to the
honey tree."

Christopher Robin handed the balloon to Pooh. Instantly the little bear began to rise into the air.

"See?" he said.

Christopher Robin grabbed onto Pooh and pulled him back down.

"Thank you," said Pooh. "Now would you be so kind as to take me to a muddy place?"

So Christopher Robin took Pooh to a very muddy place. And Pooh rolled and rolled until he was muddy all over.

"There now," said Pooh. "Isn't this a clever disguise?"

"What are you supposed to be?" asked Christopher Robin.

"A little black rain cloud, of course," replied Pooh. "Now, would you aim me at the bees, please?"

Christopher Robin let go of his friend, and up, up, up Pooh floated to the treetop.

"Pay no attention to me," Pooh said, sticking his paw
into a hole in the tree. He pulled it right out again when
a bee flew out and landed on his nose.

"I think the bees suspect something," said Pooh.

"Perhaps they think you're after their honey," called Christopher Robin.

"Well, you never can tell with bees," replied Pooh. "But I think it would help to fool the bees if you would open your umbrella and say, 'Tut, tut . . . It looks like rain.'"

So Christopher Robin opened his umbrella and pretended that a rainstorm was coming to the Hundred-Acre Wood.

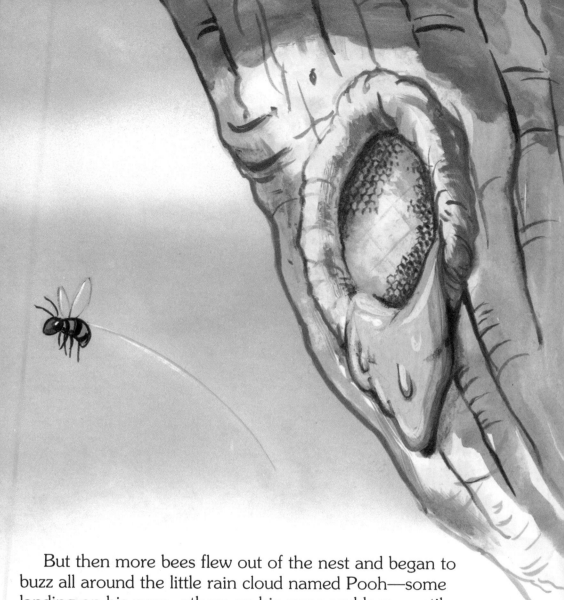

But then more bees flew out of the nest and began to buzz all around the little rain cloud named Pooh—some landing on his nose, others on his arms and legs—until he and his balloon were almost completely covered with them!

"Christopher Robin, I have come to a very important decision!" shouted Pooh. "These are the wrong sort of bees."

Just then the air started to leak out of the balloon, and Pooh began to fall.

"Oh, bother. I think I shall come down," said Pooh.

"I'll catch you," said Christopher Robin, which is just what he did.

But the bees kept coming. So the two friends took off
running through the Hundred-Acre Wood. When Pooh
tripped over a log, Christopher Robin ran back to save
him. Then together they jumped into a mud hole to hide.

Christopher Robin opened his umbrella to cover
them, and the bees flew right by. The two friends were
safe at last!

"You never can tell with bees," said Pooh.

Christopher Robin smiled at his friend and said, "Silly
old bear!"